AF595889
o

LAURA + PHILIP BUNTING

Hey, wild thing! Are you about to start school? Then it's time to get set for your wildest adventure yet. Follow this simple guide and you'll learn everything you need to know.

From teacher tips to finding friends, we've got you covered, so even the wildest little creature will settle in quickly and easily.

e
!

❶ Wakey wakey!

Start your school day with a gentle wake-up call.

Recommended:

Definitely **not** recommended:

2 Get dressed.

Ensure you are neatly and appropriately dressed for school.

Yes.

No.

Nope.

Saturday!

③ Breakfast.

Give yourself lasting energy by choosing a healthy, filling breakfast appropriate to your species.

This little koala had a **healthy breakfast**:

This little koala **did not**:

❹ School essentials.

It's a good idea to test out your equipment before your first day to make sure you know how to use it properly.

Sticky tape.

✓ Used for:
Craft, artwork, sticking stuff into your workbook.

✗ Not used for:
Turning your teacher into a sticky, grumpy mummy.

Backpack.

✓ Carrying your lunch and school equipment.
✗ Hide and seek.

Crayons.

✓ Drawing, writing and other colourful creations.
✗ Lunch.

Scissors.

✓ Chopping paper and string.
✗ Haircuts.

Protractor.

✓ Measuring your angles.
✗ Enhancing your smile.

5 First-day feelings.

Whatever your mix of emotions, you can be sure someone else is feeling exactly the same way. And those feelings are all perfectly normal.

6 The way to school.

Make your way to school safely and avoid distractions along the way.

Safe

Unsafe

Very unsafe

Ridiculous

7 Drop-off.

If you feel sad when you say goodbye, a quick farewell will make this bit much easier. Try these:

Save those big hugs for home time.

❽ Your classroom.

Your classroom is your new habitat. It's an exciting place with lots of things to make, do, and learn. Remember, if you're unsure of how to do something, just ask your teacher or a classmate.

Aa Bb Cc Dd Ee
Ff Gg Hh Ii Jj Kk
Ll Mm Nn Oo Pp
Qq Rr Ss Tt Uu
Vv Ww Xx Yy
hELLO

9 Your teacher.

No matter what their shape or species, all teachers are made up of some truly wonderful qualities.

Kindness

Enthu-siasm

Creat-ivity

Your teacher

Knowledge

Humour

Wisdom

Teacher ID.

Name. Ms Prickleback
Position. Teacher
Dept. Puggles and wuggles
Height. 27cm
Weight. 6kg, before lunch
Species. Tachyglossus aculeatus
Motto. "Stay sharp"

Issued by
Department of Anthropomorphics.

If you think *you* have a lot to think about at school, spare a thought for your teacher! Their minds are always working to make learning fun and interesting, while keeping a whole bunch of wild things safe, happy and out of trouble. Here's a peek inside the mind of a teacher ...

You will spend a lot of time with your teacher in the year ahead.

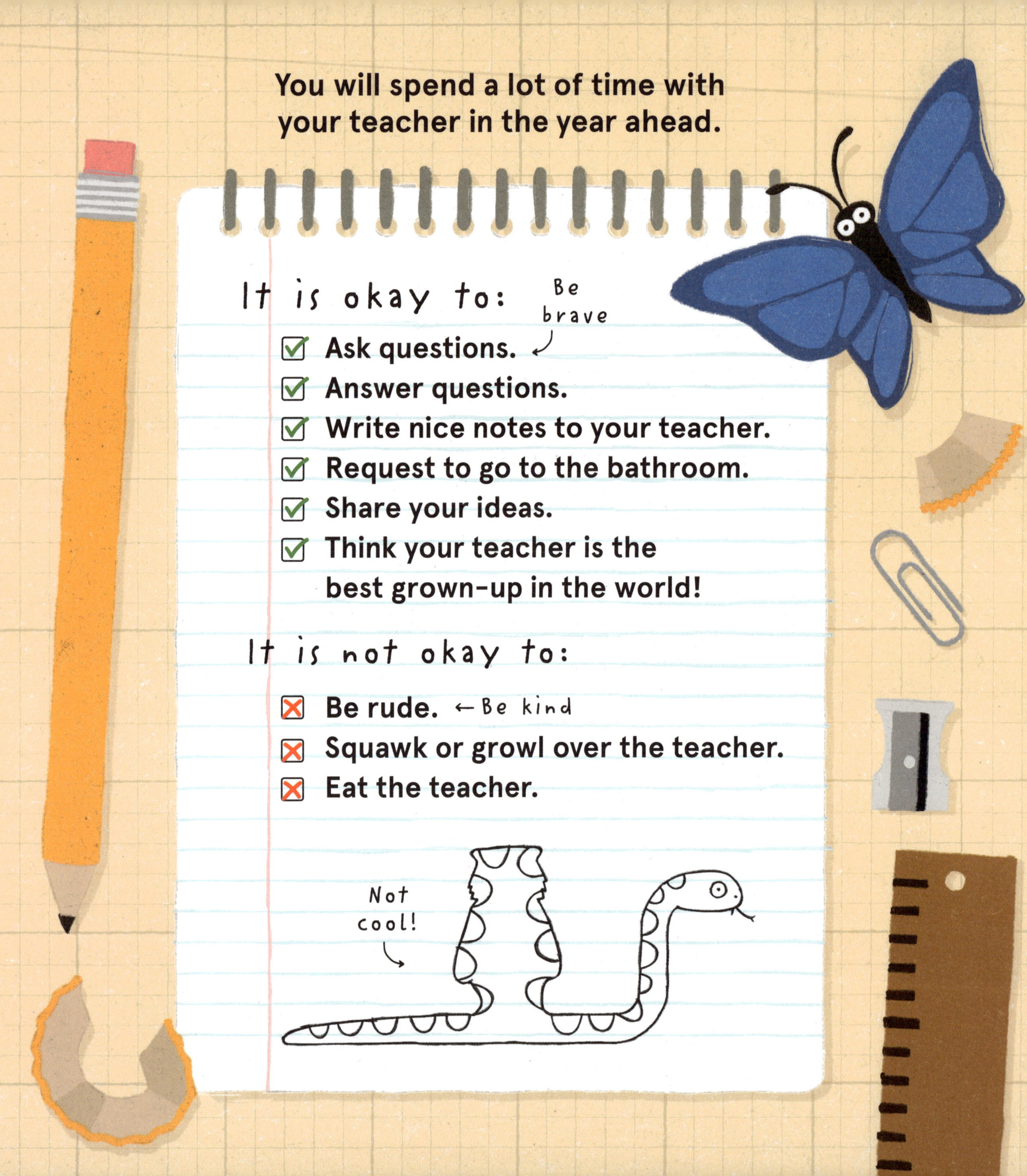

⑩ Missing home.

It's normal to miss home when you are at school, and there are lots of things you can do to make yourself feel better. Try these:

Think about the end-of-day hug.

Cuddle a class softie.

Let your teacher know you are missing home.

Put a cuddle from home in your pocket (or pouch).

⓫ How to be an eager learner.

Listening, waiting your turn, and trying your best in class will take you a long way.

Could be keener

Keen

Very keen

Too keen

12 Listening.

At school – just as it is out in the wild – listening can be more important than talking. In this example, the students at Bilby Burrow State School have been asked to draw a tree.

13 Lunch time!

Remember to pack a healthy lunch, appropriate to your species.

14 Using the toilet.

When nature calls at school, you will need to use the toilet (bush wees are not cool at school!).

✓ Always use the school toilets. Ask your teacher if you are unsure where they are.

✗ Do not poop in the blocks.

✗ Do not poop on your teacher.

15 Play time!

The playground is where you can let out some energy and go wild!

16 Making new friends.

Making a new friend can be as easy as smiling and asking a question.

Remember to smile!

Here are a few questions to try, just in case you get stuck: What's your name? • Would you like to play tag? • What's your favourite song? • Where is your nest? • Do you like to eat earthworms too?

When making new friends, try to avoid:

Pawnote: Do not poop in the sandpit.
You don't win friends with poop. See #14.

17 Home time.

(This bit's mostly for grown-ups)

Your little wildling will be tired after their first day of school. Give them a big hug and some tasty grub, or grubs, and don't worry if they don't share too much about their day.* Here is a chart of typical wildling responses to the eternal question:

"What did you do at school today?"

18 Bed time.

*It will often come to them later ...

"And then a snake almost ate a bilby,
and a bilby ate a crayon sandwich,
and a wombat pooped in the blocks,
and a galah got a terrible haircut,
and I made five new friends,
and ... and ... and ..."

Good lu

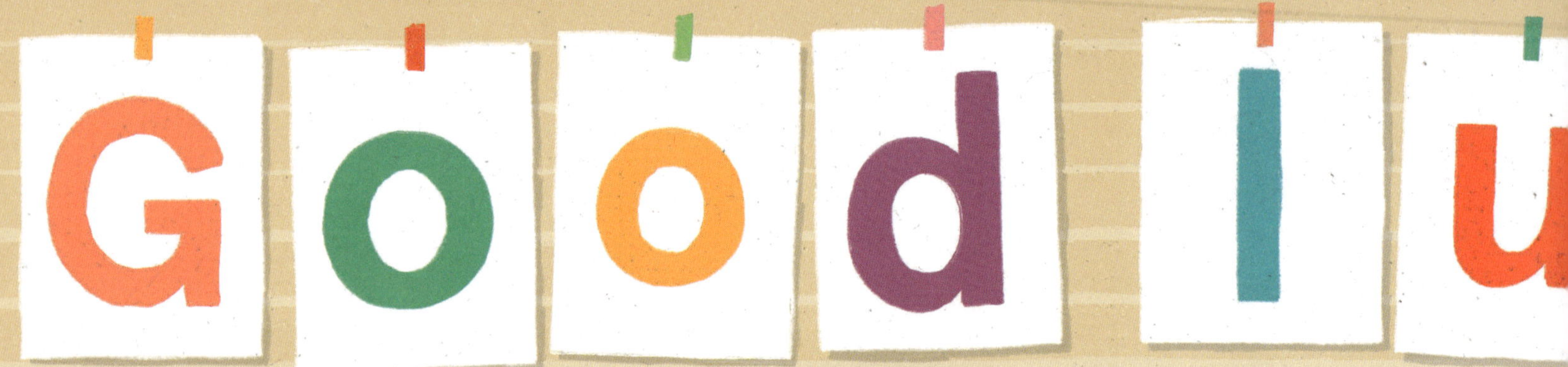

Congratulations! You now know all about your first day at school. So strap on your backpack and your smile because you are officially ready for your wildest adventure yet.

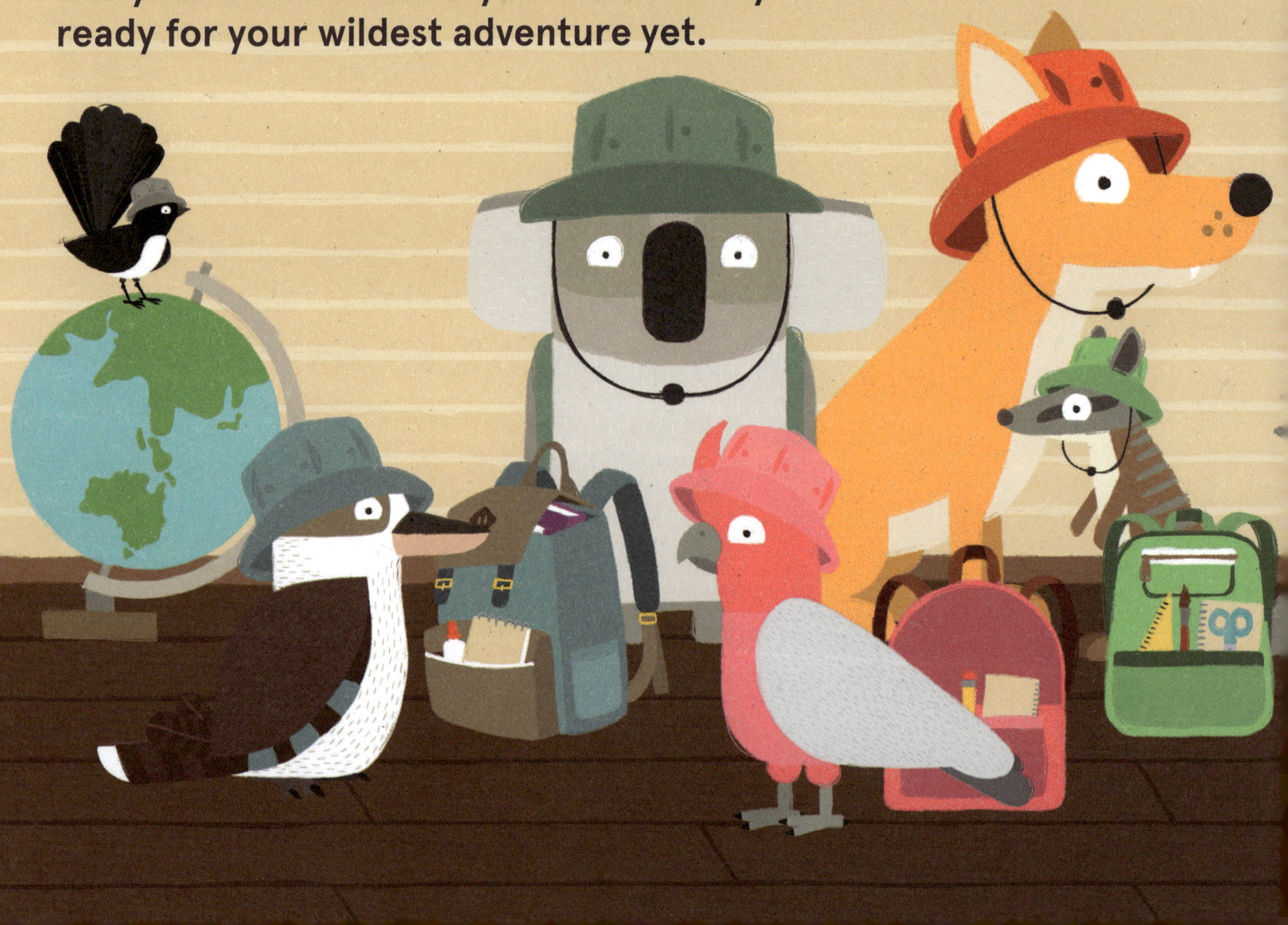

ck!

For Arthur —
the wildest one
Xx

Omnibus Books
an imprint of Scholastic Australia Pty Ltd
(ABN 11 000 614 577)
PO Box 579, Gosford NSW 2250.
www.scholastic.com.au

Part of the Scholastic Group
Sydney • Auckland • New York • Toronto • London • Mexico City •
New Delhi • Hong Kong • Buenos Aires • Puerto Rico

First published by Scholastic Australia in 2022.
This edition published in 2024.

A catalogue record for this book is available from the National Library of Australia

ISBN: 978-1-76152-129-4

Printed in China by RR Donnelley. Scholastic Australia's policy, in association with RR Donnelley, is to use papers that are renewable and made efficiently from wood grown in responsibly managed sources, so as to minimise its environmental footprint.

10 9 8 7 6 5 4 3 2 25 26 27 28 / 2

Acknowledgement of Country: We acknowledge the traditional custodians of the land on which we live and work, and pay respect to the Gubbi Gubbi nation. We pay respects to the Elders of the community and extend our recognition to their descendants. Laura and Philip Bunting.

Name:
Class:
Subject:
Name:
Class:
Subject:
Name:
Class:
Subject:
Name:
Class:
Subject:
Name:
Class:
Subject:
Name:
Class:
Subject:
Name:
Class:
Subject:
Name:
Class:
Subject:

Discover *heaps* more books
by Laura and Philip Bunting:

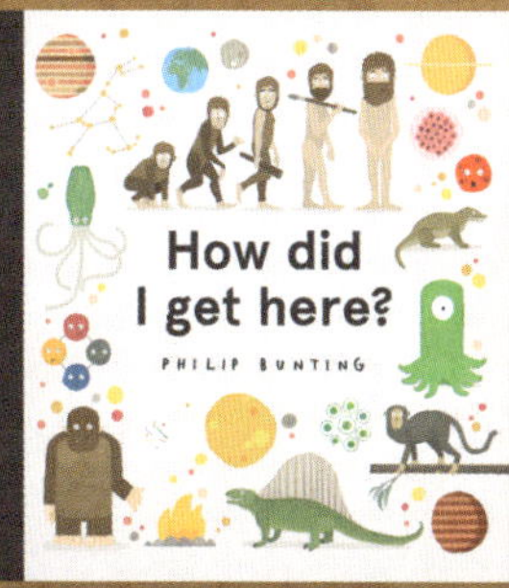